to: _____
from: _____

Evie's Christmas Wishes

Siobhán Parkinson

Shannon Bergin

Little Island

Christmas is coming.

At school, the children
are rehearsing.

'I wish I had a singing part,'
says Evie in a whisper.

At home,
Evie is helping
to make the
pudding.

'We should have
made it ages ago,'
says Daddy.
'We forgot.'

'I hope we don't forget *Christmas*,'
says Evie.

Evie and Mammy are on their way to the pantomime.

'I wish we had a reindeer,' says Evie.

Evie and Mammy are decorating
the Christmas cake.

They put a robin on it and
sprinkle it with silver stars.

'I hope it tastes as good
as it looks,' says Evie.

Uncle Seán is coming home for Christmas.

He says he has a big surprise.

It might be a scooter, Evie thinks.

Daddy has brought the
Christmas decorations
down from the attic.

Evie is in charge of decorating the tree.

'Oh, look!
A reindeer!'
she says.

Evie is writing to Santa Claus. She'd like a train and a doll's house and a chemistry set and ...

'I wish I had a baby sister,'
says Evie in a whisper.

At school, it's the Christmas play.

Evie is a shepherd with a shepherd's crook,
and she gets to sing along as well.

Evie's friend's little brother
is the baby in the manger.

The weather forecast says it will be
a wet and windy Christmas.

'I wish it could be a *white* Christmas,'
says Evie in a whisper.

Evie is helping Mammy with the crib.

'Am I called after Christmas Eve?'
asks Evie.

'For sure,' says Mammy.

Carol singers have come to the door.

'Can you sing the one with the angels?'
Daddy asks.

'I wish we had an angel,'
says Evie in a whisper.

On Christmas Eve it snows, all soft and sparkly.

Evie is putting a candle in the window for later.

'It wasn't *supposed* to be a white Christmas!' she says.

Mammy and Daddy and Evie
are waiting for Uncle Seán.

car park P

rtures

'I wonder what the surprise will be,' says Daddy to Evie.

'Maybe it'll be a *pony*,' says Evie.

Suddenly Uncle Seán is there and Daddy is hugging and hugging and hugging him.

Mrs Uncle Seán is there too, only her real name is Tessa and she is lovely.

But she is not the surprise.

The *baby* is the surprise.

Her name is Angel.

She is the best Christmas surprise *ever*.